Greg's Tall Tales

by Liza Charlesworth

ISBN: 978-1-338-89042-6

Designer: Cynthia Ng; Illustrated by John Lund

Copyright © 2023 by Liza Charlesworth. All rights reserved. Published by Scholastic Inc.

1 2 3 4 5 6 7 8 9 10   68   31 30 29 28 27 26 25 24 23 22

Printed in Jiaxing, China. First printing, January 2023.

■SCHOLASTIC

Once upon a time,
there was a giant named Greg.
He was big, tall, and strong.
But his life was small, calm, and ordinary.
Greg watched very nice TV shows.

Greg read very nice books.
Greg went for very nice walks
in the very nice park
in his very nice town.

Everything about Greg's life was very nice.
And that made him sad. Why?
All of Greg's pals thought he had
a BIG life full of adventure…
but he did NOT.

"Hi Greg!" said his pal Ann.
"I can't wait to hear what you did today!"
The truth was that Greg had sat on a bench
and watched a squirrel climb a tree.
But that was too boring for a giant.

5

So Greg made up a tall tale.
"I met a huge purple squirrel.
Then, we swung on some vines," he said.
"Wow, your life is amazing!" replied Ann.

"Hi Greg!" said his pal Rick.
"I can't wait to hear what you did today!"
The truth was that Greg had gone to the market
and bought some vegetables.
But that was too boring for a giant.

So Greg made up a tall tale.
"I met a fancy blue dinosaur by the carrots.
Then, I went to his cave for tea," said Greg.
"Wow, your life is amazing!" replied Rick.

"Hi Greg!" said his pal Kim.
"I can't wait to hear what you did today!"
The truth was Greg had put on his sneakers
and gone for a short jog.
But that was too boring for a giant.

So Greg made up a tall tale.
"I put on my magic sneakers and
jumped right over a house," he said.
"Wow, your life is amazing!" said Kim.

Then she added, "My life is SO boring.
Can I take a picture of you jumping
over that bus to show my friends?"
"Well…um…er…ugh!" replied Greg.
Greg was caught in a lie, so he started to cry.

"What's wrong, Greg?" asked Kim.
"My sneakers aren't magic.
I didn't jump over a house," he replied.
"I told a tall tale to make my life seem exciting...
because it's really quite boring."

Kim felt sorry for her pal.

"Greg, don't be sad," she said.

"It's not right to tell tall tales,

but your imagination IS amazing.

Have you ever tried writing stories?"

Wow, Greg liked Kim's idea A LOT!
So he ran home and sat down at his desk.
Then, he took out a new pencil
and began to write and write and write.

Greg wrote about a huge purple squirrel.
Greg wrote about a fancy blue dinosaur.
Greg even wrote about a giant in magic sneakers
who could jump over a house.

Greg put all of his stories in a thick book.
And guess what? Everyone LOVED them!
Greg became the BIGGEST writer in the world…
and that's no tall tale.